Carnal Moon

Wicked Fate Lusty Mates

Astrid Vail

Rogue Queen Publishing

Carnal Moon

Copyright © 2024 by Astrid Vail & Rogue Queen Publishing

All rights reserved. No part of this book may be used or reproduced, stored or transmitted in any form or by any means, electronic, mechanical, photocopying, recording, scanning, or otherwise in any manner whatsoever without written permission except in the case of brief quotations bodied in critical articles or reviews.

It is illegal to copy this book, post it on a website, or distribute it by any means without permission.

This book is a work of fiction. Names, characters, businesses, organizations, places, events, and incidents either are the product of the author's imagination or are used fictitiously. Any resemblance to actual persons, living or dead, events, or locales is entirely coincidental.

Cover Art by GetCovers

Edited by NiceGirlNaughtyEdits

First Edition: January 2024

ISBN

eBook : 978-1-958641-22-4

Paperback: 978-1-958641-23-1

Content warning includes steamy on page sex scenes, primal chase, and language.

This author does not use AI in their writing or cover art.

Contents

Blurb & Content Warning	IV
1. Chapter One	1
2. Chapter Two	9
3. Chapter Three	16
4. Chapter Four	23
5. Chapter Five	29
6. Chapter Six	34
7. Chapter Seven	42
8. Chapter Eight	49
9. Chapter Nine	56
Want More ?	64
Also By Astrid Vail	65
About Astrid Vail	67

Blurb & Content Warning

Enter a new world of desire with a coven of misfit witches and the steamy discovery of their lycanthrope mates in this brand-new series by Astrid Vail.

Standing in a room full of lycanthropes, on the night of an exclusive event, is the last place Lily ever thought she would find herself.

To make matters even more complicated, she finds herself in the arms of the extremely handsome pack alpha, just the man and wolf, she came to speak with on behalf of her coven.

Only he is seductively whispering that she is his mate and has no plans on letting her go.

The only problem...

Witches and Lycanthropes are supposed to be age-old enemies, not mates.

CARNAL MOON

This novella is intended for mature readers only. **Content warning** includes steamy on page sex scenes, primal chase, and language.

Chapter One

LILY

"Lily, I still think you should let me come with you. Or better yet, I can go in your place."

Lily shook her head and tucked her hands farther under her thighs. She didn't want to show her best friend and coven member how nervous she really was by picking at her nails. "Silina, you know why I volunteered. Out of everyone in our coven, I am the least witchy. You, on the other hand, would probably get mauled after one sniff."

Silina side-eyed her before glancing out her car window at the wrought-iron gates across the road. "I still don't like leaving you here without any means of leaving."

"It's called legs and feet. I can walk out of there at any time. Plus, I have my phone."

"But—"

"No, this is happening. It's an opportunity we can't pass up. Our head priestess has been trying to get into contact with the pack alpha for a while now. This party gets me in front of him, so I can plead our case."

Silina sighed and tapped her hand against the steering wheel of her little hatchback. "I know you are right; I just don't like you going in there without anyone to watch your back. You can't even..."

She trailed off and Lily finished her sentence for her. "I can't do magic. I'm powerless. I know. That is why I'm the best person to do this."

"Rely on your instincts, Lily. And you're not powerless, you have a banging body. Men think with their dick nine times out of ten, so use it to your advantage if you need to get out of trouble. It doesn't matter if they're human, lycanthropes, or mages. They are all the same."

Lily choked slightly at Silina's words but didn't say anything. There wasn't enough time tonight to unpack *that* baggage. Silina might be her best friend in the coven and outside of it, but Lily knew relatively nothing about her past.

She took a deep breath and glanced at the clock on the dashboard. It was nearing ten p.m., and if she was really going to go through with this plan, she had to get going. She reached out and hugged Silina. "I promise I'll trust my gut. And if anything happens, I know you will come to my rescue."

Silina hugged her back. "I'm off from the club tonight. So yes, please call me if you need anything."

"And you won't wait here all night in the car."

"No promises," Silina murmured.

Lily let her comment slide as she released the hug and opened the door. The night was quiet, the waxing moon hanging high in the starless sky. It was slightly pink. A good omen. And it soothed Lily's nerves a little bit. The moon called to her in a way Lily suspected it called to the Lycans, if only on a smaller scale.

Except she wasn't a Lycan.

She was a witch.

Lily took a deep breath and focused her gaze on the wrought-iron gate in front of her. She shoved her shaking hands into her coat pocket, her fingers grazing the ticket the coven had bought collectively for this moment. She closed her eyes, trying to calm her racing heart. This had been her idea, after all, and she couldn't back out now. She had to do it for her coven, to find a way to speak to the biggest supernatural community in the city and not be shut out. And this was the easiest way to meet with *him.*

The alpha of the biggest Lycan pack in their city.

Resolve steeled her spine as Lily strode across the road, putting one heeled boot in front of the other. Far too soon for her liking, she was front and center. Reaching out, she pushed the buzzer.

Crackling of the intercom connecting seemed too loud for the night, and a shiver ran down Lily's spine as a growl echoed forth. "Name?"

Gulping, mouth suddenly going dry, she coughed, "Lilian Page."

The intercom clicked, and the gates slid open, rustling the fallen leaves surrounding it. Lily hurried through, her boots clicking against the asphalt drive.

Fear pulled at her deep inside. *It wasn't too late,* her inner monologue screamed. She could leave. She could walk right back out that gate and Silina wouldn't say a word. She would back her claim to tell her coven the alpha wouldn't see her. Wouldn't speak to her about such nonsense of treaties and abolishing old traditions to usher forth new ones. A world where witches and Lycans held hands and skipped through fields of daisies.

Lily snorted, and her fear faded slightly.

Okay, those weren't exactly the words the high priestess used, but the image in her mind set her at ease. Quickly glancing behind her, she caught Silina still sitting there in the car. She had a phone out and her feet propped out of the window.

"Silina," she hissed and made a shooing motion with her hands.

Silina responded with her middle finger, and Lily shook her head. There was nothing she could do about her staying out here all night, so she turned and continued along the drive. She followed the sound of music and boisterous laughter, up toward the sprawling estate dead ahead.

By the time Lily made it to the front steps of the main house, she was sweating. Why on goddess's green earth did the invite specifically request all guests to be dropped off at the front gates? It just seemed cruel and unusual to make someone walk up the winding drive. And in heels, nonetheless. Then again, many of the guests were probably lycanthropes, which meant they were in way better shape than she was.

Lily winced and hobbled forward, almost tripping up the four steps to the open front door. She wanted to kick off her shoes and just sit. To take a quick breather before marching into a house full of Lycans. She bit her lip, almost contemplating it, but she was already late. The party would be in full swing by now and she had to grab the attention of the alpha before midnight fell. Because there was no way Lily planned to stay around for the second part of the evening.

She made it two steps inside the foyer before a stylishly clad woman in a suit and heels stepped into view. The woman in question bowed, and before Lily could stop herself, she bowed as well. A burning sensation of a flush engulfing her whole body hit Lily immediately, and the woman cocked her head. Fear bubbled below her breastbone as the woman's nostrils flared, scenting the air. Lily gulped and hoped she didn't smell too witchy. Which was one of the main reasons why she volunteered for this task. She was more likely to pass the sniff test than anyone else in her coven. The woman smiled and extended a hand. "Ticket, please?"

Lily's heart pounded away in her chest as she scrambled for the ticket shoved in her coat pocket. She thrust it out like a madwoman, visibly shaking. Goddess be, this really was a bad idea. But it was her bad idea, and she had to see it through. The woman's lips twitched, as if she were suppressing a smile, but Lily couldn't be sure.

"Follow me, please," the woman chirped and turned on her heel. Lily nodded, even though the woman was already striding away. She hurried after her, only to slide to a stop in front of two doors. Next to the doors was a rack of black garment bags.

She briefly wondered why it would just be sitting in the hallway when a party was clearly in full swing in the house. The woman faced her once more and extended a hand. "Jacket and purse."

Lily shrugged off her jacket and small purse, handing them over to the woman before pulling at the hem of her tight dark blue pencil skirt. Along with the silver silken blouse she wore, Lily knew the outfit accentuated her curves just right. The ticket had said the party was themed, Suits and Bunnies, but Lily had no idea what the bunny part was about, so she settled on semi-formal sexy. She had even left the blouse slightly undone so the sheer lacy top underneath could peek out. Silina had called the look "office sexy." Yet the look the woman was giving Lily right now made her realize she might be underdressed for the occasion. "Ummm..." Lily wiped her sweaty hands against her skirt. "Do I look okay?"

The woman grabbed one of the black clothing bags. "Doesn't matter what you came in wearing. We have a strict dress code for this event. And you are definitely not a suit." She thrust out the bag in Lily's direction and pointed toward one of the small doors. "You can change in there. Your articles of clothing will be out here when you leave."

To demonstrate her point, the woman opened the door and a closet full of attire and coats greeted her. She pulled out a hanger and attached Lily's coat and purse before placing them in the closet. She motioned to the other door again, and Lily glanced at the mysterious garment bag in her hands. The label on the outside sported the number fourteen, and Lily arched her eyebrow. "How did you know my dress size?"

The woman dazzled Lily with a smile. "It's a special talent of mine. Now, please change, while I find a set of appropriate heels for you." She motioned to the door again.

Lily glanced down at her knee-high black leather boots with their chunky heels and sighed. The woman was probably right, and the shoes she was wearing were not going to go well with whatever was in the garment bag. Lily gave the woman a shy smile and whispered, "I'm a size nine in shoes."

The woman nodded but didn't say anything, clearly waiting for Lily to go into the mysterious room to change. Seeing as this was going to be the only way of getting into the party and fulfilling the task she volunteered for, Lily turned quickly and opened the door, stepping inside. Her jaw dropped as she realized the room wasn't just a simple changing room, but a powder room. Decorated in an eggshell and light mint color scheme, Lily stifled her laugh of disbelief. There was even gold speckling around the sink and on the floor tiles. It was gaudy and rich and everything Lily loathed. She scanned the rest of the room and shook her head. "Unbelievable."

She turned around and draped her garment bag on the hook bolted to the door. Unzipping the bag quickly, she stared in equal amounts of shock and horror. Compared to this outfit, the powder room was relatively tame. Her hand reached out of its own accord, stroking the dark silk scrap of fabric in front of her. A flush overcoming her body encased her from head to toe. This was almost too much, but she steeled her spine and slowly extracted the corseted bodice and barely-there mini skirt she knew wouldn't fully cover her ass. A pair of silken white bunny ears, along with a fluffy white tail, fell from the bag onto the floor. Lily cursed. "You have got to be fucking kidding me."

Chapter Two

HUNTER

HUNTER DIDN'T WANT TO be here.

Except this was his house, his late family's estate, and tonight was his year to host this ridiculous Suits and Bunnies event. The first part of the event allowed those in attendance to sniff each other out and if they wanted to, move onto the second part of the evening. A nice little primal chase through the woods. Exactly the thing Hunter wanted on his property.

A nice forest sex party.

Not.

He groaned inside. Hunter liked to live a more secluded life. He kept his pack in line, was a leading force on the supernatural council, and enjoyed his solitude. Which was something he really wished he had right now. Instead, his senses were on high alert as he watched the party goers mill about, a mixing of Lycans from various packs and a spattering of humans brave enough to show up. There were no other supernatural's present and Hunter was relieved. His species was high-strung, dangerous, and very territorial. Lycans rarely got along with others besides humans. Maybe because they had more in common with their human half than with their wolfish brethren?

Hunter mused over his philosophical thoughts, barely paying attention to the Lycan speaking to him, when he smelled it. The biting scent of magic. It was faint, oh so faint, but he picked it up all the same. Sweet and tart and absolutely captivating. His eyes darted around the room until he spotted the culprit.

His mouth watered instantly as he eyed the witch, who dared to enter a den full of Lycans.

A voluptuous beauty with a waterfall of dark ruby-red hair and creamy skin stood awkwardly in the middle of the room. She wore a ridiculous rabbit costume designated for the bunnies at the party. Except it didn't look so ridiculous on *her*. The corseted black bodice with white stitching hugged her curves, barely containing her luscious breasts. She tugged at the silk mini skirt, trying to keep her round ass from falling out. Hunter couldn't stop staring, his eyes roaming from the silly bunny tail she was wearing all the way up to the equally silly ears. Fuck, he wanted to chase her down and rut with her right in the middle of the dining room. He wondered how she would sound with him behind her, driving his throbbing cock into her warm pussy. Or better yet, with his face buried between her legs. She could even keep the bunny ears on; they looked cute on her.

The Lycan he was speaking to tilted his head to the side, following his gaze. The man's intake of breath made Hunter want to rip him to shreds. Actually, he wanted to rip this entire room to shreds, killing all who dared.

Oh shit.

This was not good.

Hunter barely processed his heightened emotions and the meaning behind them before someone approached *his* redheaded beauty. He snarled as the person in question pointed right at her face, crowding her in. Her beautiful features scrunched in panic, and she took a step away from the man, hands held up in defense.

The redhead teetered on the stupid stiletto heels she was wearing and crashed into Hunter's chest. His breathing had turned ragged in the few seconds it had taken him to make his way over. Yet feeling the redhead pushed against him calmed his racing pulse.

She would be safe now. Now that he was here to protect her.

Hunter linked his arm around her ribcage, right under her breasts, and pulled her in closer. His movement made her tits jiggle in the most enticing way, and it was a struggle to pull his eyes away from them. Yet he managed, barely.

His gaze followed the dip of her collarbone and up her slender neck to her face. Her full, lush lips were parted in surprise, and when he finally met her eyes, his breath caught. Those pretty hazel eyes would be the death of him. He reached up to trail his fingers across his redhead's racing pulse before whispering, "You're safe now."

The redhead opened her mouth before shutting it quickly, her eyes darting across his face frantically. She finally glanced away and to the man standing in front of her.

Oh yes. The waste of space harassing her. He should probably get rid of him.

He tore his eyes away from his redhead and focused his stare on the Lycan in question. "Who are you?"

The Lycan tried to meet his gaze, but it was impossible unless he was an alpha like Hunter. In the end, he settled a loathing stare at Hunter's redheaded beauty. "Alpha Hunter, my name is Derek, and the woman you are claiming to protect is a witch."

The redhead in Hunter's arms visibly flinched from the malice in the Lycan's voice. Which only made him squeeze her tighter to his frame. Fuck, she could probably feel how hard he was right now. Shit... Her short skirt had slid up when he grabbed her. Dropping his hand to her thick, warm thigh, he pulled it back into place. She was his, and no one was going to see her assets but him.

The redhead squeaked as his hand snaked around her thigh, and Hunter buried his head in her neck and breathed in deeply. He chuckled softly and nipped her skin before lifting his head and gazing at the Lycan before them. "She is but a little witch with barely any power. She isn't causing any trouble, unlike you."

Derek's face turned red as he sputtered, "Alpha Hunter, you don't understand. She's a double-crossing cu—"

Hunter moved, hand wrapping around Derek's throat before he could finish his sentence. "Watch your tone while in my house, you useless excuse for a Lycan."

Derek struggled feebly before giving up and muttering, "Apologies, Alpha Hunter."

Hunter growled and jerked his head. "Don't apologize to me. Apologize to..."

He trailed off as the redhead wiggled and slipped from his embrace. She glanced between the two of them, cheeks stained a rosy pink. "I'm... I'm... I shouldn't have come here," she stuttered before spinning on her flimsy heels and running out of the room.

Hunter's low growl reverberated through his chest as he watched his little bunny run away from him. He wanted... no, *needed* to go after her, but a crowd was gathering around them. He glared at Derek and shoved him away. The useless waste of space fell to the ground, rubbing at his throat. A bruise was already forming on his neck, but he would be fine, unfortunately.

Lycans healed fast.

Derek coughed, clearing his throat. "Alpha Hunter. I know this witch, and she can't be—"

Hunter cut him off with a swipe of his hand. "Get out of my house."

"But... but I came here to pension—"

Hunter roared, "I don't care who you are or why you are here. Get. Out. Of. My. House."

Derek scrambled and ran toward the outer doors. Thankfully, not the ones the redheaded beauty had left through. The crowd whispered and departed, the clinking of glasses and awkward laughter filling the room once more.

Hunter stalked over to the bar and gulped down a glass of water. He was drinking his third glass when a presence made herself known by his right side.

"Well... that was interesting, Alpha Brother."

Hunter glanced over to the female Lycan, his twin sister, to be exact. She gave him a wolfish smile as she leaned back against the bar top. "Is she still here?"

His sister laughed and grabbed the glass of water out of his hand. She twirled the glass like it held a fine whiskey instead of water as she glanced over the room of people. "Yes, Brother. The witch is still here. I followed her. She is in the lady's room, probably calming down after that hedonistic display of power you just demonstrated."

Hunter growled and grabbed the water back from his twin and gulped it down. He glanced at the long mirror behind the wall before looking away quickly. His normal brown eyes glinted with amber flecks, the sight of his wolf peeking out from within. He needed to calm down before he went after his redheaded witch.

"I want you on her all night until I calm down my wolf."

The purr that came from Hunter's sister could have rivaled that of any cat shifter. "Gladly."

Hunter grabbed her by the arm, territorial rage almost blinding him. "Sister, please."

She scoffed and rolled her eyes before peeling his fingers off her arm. "I'm just playing. I won't make any moves on your pretty little witch."

Hunter sighed in relief, and his twin pushed away from the bar. He watched her go and took a deep breath before focusing his thoughts inward to tame his wayward wolf.

His Lycan half howled at him, and he reassured his beast that they would claim the witch soon enough. He just had to figure out a way to convince his bunny that she was his.

Because there was only one logical reason behind the way he and his wolf felt in this moment.

The little witch was his mate.

Chapter Three

LILY

"Breathe. Just breathe. Everything will be fine if you just breathe."

Lily gripped the edge of the porcelain sink so hard she thought it might crack. A mix of embarrassment, rage, and lust flowed through her. Lily really, really wanted to dismiss that last feeling. Goddess above, she cannot be lusting after the sexy Lycan, the alpha of the pack her high priestess wanted Lily to make negotiations with. And she really needed to stop thinking about the way his arms felt when he wrapped them around her. The way he put his face in her neck and growled…

Nope. Most definitely shouldn't be thinking about that.

She glanced into the mirror and gritted her teeth.

"Breathe in. One. Two. Three. Breathe out. One. Two. Three," Lily murmured to herself over and over until she could finally think. The flush covering her face and chest finally dissipated, just as the sound of heels coming closer registered. The doorknob rattled, and Lily called out. "Occupied."

"No shit. Let me in. We need to talk."

Lily blinked, the woman's honeyed growl filling the small bathroom she had locked herself in. "Ummmm... I think you have the wrong person."

The woman on the other side of the door snorted. "No, I most definitely have the right person, little witch."

Panic bubbled under her breastbone and Lily glanced around franticly. There was no way out besides the door in front of her, which looked flimsy now that an angry Lycan female stood on the other side.

"Little witch, my brother sent me to watch you. Now open the damn door before I huff and puff and blow it down."

Lily bit her lip, and with the last ounce of bravery swimming through her veins, she reached forward, and unlocked the door. It creaked open slowly and the female Lycan peered in with a look of surprise on her face. Like she was already planning on breaking down the door and was shocked her threat worked. Lily gave her a hesitant wave and an awkward smile. "Please don't kill me." The female scoffed before stepping inside and shutting the door behind her. She threw the lock and gave Lily a toothy grin.

Lily's grip on the sink tightened once more.

Shit. The Lycan female *was* totally going to kill her.

Hysterical laughter tried to escape as Lily thought about what a mess her death would make. Blood splattered all over the nice mint and eggshell bathroom. She really hated that the colors in the bathroom matched the powder room she was in earlier this evening. A hiccup forced its way out and Lily slapped her hand over her mouth.

The Lycan female gave Lily an odd look and tilted her head, almost as if she was listening. After a moment, she whispered, "Okay, good. No eavesdroppers are present. I'm Sasha, and my brother really, really likes you. Which means I like you. No murder, I promise." She reached out and pulled Lily's hand away from the sink and shook it.

"I'm Li... Li... Lily."

She managed to stammer her name, eyes going wide. The fear of dying dissipated and she glanced at her hand, still being shaken in an ecstatic manner. Now that Sasha mentioned it, she did look vaguely like the Lycan who had rescued her earlier. She sported the same light tan skin, golden brown hair, and caramel brown eyes. They even had the same bone structure, except Sasha had more feminine features. Though, she was taller than her brother.

Lily glanced down quickly. No, they were the same height. She was wearing stilettos. Just like Lily's, except Sasha looked a lot better in them with her outfit. Lily extracted her hand, and the words tumbled unbidden from her mouth. "Why do you get to wear a sexy pantsuit while all the other ladies are wearing *this* in random colors?"

Lily gestured to herself, and Sasha chuckled before turning to the mirror. She pulled out a tube of liquid red lipstick and started touching up her lips. "Because," she murmured, and Sasha's reflection winked at Lily, "I'm a predator. Not the prey. And there were a few other women out there wearing similar outfits to mine. You just missed them while successfully seducing my brother."

Lily gulped and shook her head as Sasha put the finishing touches on her lips and fluffed her long, curly hair. "I wasn't... I wouldn't... I didn't come here to seduce anyone. I'm sorry I made trouble out there. I was just about to leave, anyway. This was an absolute failure."

Sasha turned slowly, her gaze racking Lily up and down. "You're leaving?"

Lily nodded and hugged herself. "I shouldn't have even shown up. It was a stupid plan."

"Plan?" Sasha echoed.

"Yes, plan. The high priestess has been trying, unsuccessfully, I might add, to speak with the Lycan council. We... I know that witches and Lycans have a tumultuous relationship, but my high priestess wants to... thinks that...." Lily trailed off and shook her head. "I swear I had a whole spiel memorized."

Sasha's lip curled slightly. "Why didn't your high priestess just come herself? Seems cowardly to send you. By yourself, I might add."

Lily gulped and looked down at her feet. "It was my idea. I don't have any power. I have no witchy abilities, so I came here thinking..."

"That you could seduce an alpha without him knowing you were a witch?"

"What! No!" Lily squeaked out and shook her head violently. "I just thought because I don't have power, it wouldn't be seen as invading his territory and I might be able to speak to Gabriel..."

"Hunter," Sasha murmured.

"Er... I mean, Hunter, about possibly speaking to the council on behalf of the coven. But your brother is very busy and is rarely seen in public. And when I saw this event was open to the public, I took a chance at possibly trying the catch his attention."

Lily was panting by the end of her little speech, sweat pooling in places she really didn't want to think about. Great, now she was stinky *and* embarrassed. Wait... Lily frowned. "I thought the alpha's name was Gabriel."

Sasha shook her head. "He prefers to go by his last name."

Lily felt her curiosity take over, but she pushed it down. She didn't need to know why; she just needed to get out of this place. She stared at the expensive gold-flecked tile on the bathroom floor, wishing she was at home vegging out on her comfy couch, eating popcorn, instead of here, stuffed into heels that hurt her feet.

Sasha cleared her throat, and Lily glanced at her. "Who was that Lycan my brother saved you from, anyway? He was a complete douche bag, and I really, really want to kick his ass."

Lily rasped out a laugh and shook her head. "He was someone from my past, from when I first moved here three years ago. We met at a café, and he wouldn't take no for an answer when he asked me out on a date. I finally just gave in and went out to coffee with him. I didn't know he was a Lycan at the time, but once I found out, I told him I was a witch. He was not pleased, to say the least."

Sasha's lip curled up, a growl reverberating from her chest. "That's it. I'm kicking his ass if I ever see him again. This thing between witches and Lycans is old and pointless. A feud that doesn't even make sense anymore."

Lily exhaled a sigh of relief. "I agree. I'm so glad you and your brother agree."

Sasha smirked. "Well, Lily, I think you accomplished your coven's plan. You will most definitely be seeing much more of Hunter again."

Lily frowned. "What do you mean?"

Sasha gave her an innocent look, yet what tumbled out of her mouth was anything but.

"The only time a Lycan acts the way my brother did earlier with a virtual stranger is when that stranger is their mate."

Lily's mouth dropped, and she stared at Sasha in disbelief. She tried to make words come out, but the only thing rattling around in her mind was the word *mate*.

Sasha reached out and unlocked the bathroom door. "Welcome to the family, Little Witch."

Lily was still reeling from the bombshell dropped on her. She flinched as the door closed behind Sasha and she was once again alone in the bathroom. "Mate?" Lily whispered, staring at the mirror. "How could I be a Lycan's mate?"

She stared at her shocked expression reflected in the mirror. Lifting both of her hands, she pressed them against her cheeks. Her skin, only moments before flushed, had become cold and clammy. She shook her head and kicked off her shoes quickly. Picking them up, she dashed out of the bathroom and down the side hall, avoiding the few questions gazes pointed her way. Once she skidded out into the large foyer, she made her way back to the woman who had greeted her barely an hour before. She shoved the heels in her direction. "I need to leave. Can I have my stuff, please?"

The woman nodded before her eyes went wide, looking over Lily's shoulder. She gulped, and Lily didn't need to turn around to know that Gabriel Hunter, Alpha of the Southern Moon pack, was standing right behind her.

Chapter Four

LILY

Lily turned in slow motion, her mind bouncing between one of two scenarios. This was either the start of a badly written horror movie or a porno. Her eyes grazed Hunter's face and her heart beat wildly as he prowled closer. Heat pooled low in her abdomen, her body betraying the feeling she was trying to hide. Fuck, he was sexy as sin.

Porno alert, her mind screamed, and Lily started sweating again. Her mind filtered through two words. Porno. Mate.

Porno.

Mate.

"Seriously, get a fucking grip," Lily muttered, and Hunter paused barely a foot away from her. The blush that was heating Lily's chest and face burned hotter. Shit, she had said that out loud. Well, at least it was better than saying *porno* or *mate* out loud. Lily was still gazing at Hunter's perfectly chiseled face, and it was an effort to avert her gaze. Hunter tilted his head, eyes grazing over Lily's shoulder. She turned her head to see the woman she had all but forgotten about. The head tilt must have been Lycan code to scamper away, because that was just what the woman did.

Hunter took a deep breath and held it for a moment. "Here, let me help you."

Lily shivered, even though she was burning up, as Hunter grabbed her long coat and placed it over her shoulders. He held on to it as she quickly placed her arms through the sleeves. She held her breath as his fingers moved quickly over the buttons. Grabbing her heeled boots, he knelt, his hands hot as a brand against her bare calf. Lily bit her lip to suppress a whimper as he lifted her foot and placed the boot on. She swayed slightly and grabbed his shoulders for support. Her mind splintered into a myriad of wicked thoughts as she felt his hard muscles move under her hands. He finished putting on her other boot and stood. Lily's hands slid from his shoulders to rest on his chest. She stared at him, mouth slightly agape. "Thank you."

Hunter reached out, his fingers slightly caressing her skin as he moved a lock of her hair away from her face and tucked it behind her ear. "Little Witch, I had hoped you would stay a little longer. You brighten up this drab party."

"You... you can call me Li... Lily," she stammered out while staring at his perfect lips.

Hunter smiled and leaned closer. Lily gulped, torn between pushing away or clutching his shirt. Insanity on her part seemed to win out as her hands gripped him closer. Hunter's lips scrapped against her ear. "I wish you were staying, Lily. It would be a pleasure to see what would happen between the two of us once midnight strikes."

His words made Lily pull away, doubt and uncertainty making her commonsense return. This had to be an elaborate ruse to get into her panties. This couldn't be real. "I'm sure you say that to all the ladies."

Hunter blinked slowly, as if stunned, and Lily mentally chastised herself. Great. She just called the Alpha of a Lycan pack a floozie. She was supposed to be helping her coven, trying to get an Alpha to take a meeting with their High Priestess. And she was most definitely not supposed to walk away from this party with a Lycan as a mate. Lily gulped, her throat parched, as if she had just run a mile and she realized they were just staring at each other. Her eyes grew wide as Hunter grazed his fingertips down her neck, placing his hand on her rapidly beating pulse. She made a noise, somewhere between a whimper and a gasp, before quickly taking a step away.

Hunter let his hand fall and Lily took another step back. "I, ummm... I should, I need..." Holy shit, she was a mess. "I, uhhh..."

She took another step back, angling toward the door. Hunter's eyes glowed amber as he watched her walk away, his body tense. She had almost made it to the door when he finally spoke. "I've never participated in a primal chase. Never interested me until now. Not until I gazed upon you."

Her heart skittered in her chest, and she wanted to curse at him. Was he saying this wasn't a stupid prank? That she, a powerless witch, was somehow special?

It was just too hard to accept. He was a Lycan, and she was a witch.

The word mate came to the forefront of her mind, and she shook it away. Now that she had put a few feet of distance between them, she could think a little better. "Your... your sister said I was your mate. I can't be your mate. You don't really want me. I'm just a powerless witch, no one of any consequence."

Then again, maybe her brain was still mush. Why had she just blurted out her greatest shame to this relative stranger?

A growl reverberated through the foyer, and Hunter stalked forward, pinning her between the door and his arms. She should have been petrified, yet her body betrayed her, arousal running through her bloodstream instead. She titled her chin up so she could gaze into Hunter's eyes. "You're wrong," he whispered.

"What?"

"You're not of no consequence. You are mine, and I am yours."

She wet her lips, swallowing the words she wanted to say. She wanted to say witches and Lycans were timeless enemies. That he should be interested in one of the classier women milling around inside the party. Not her, a self-proclaimed couch potato. Plus, he was an Alpha. He needed a strong mate, not someone like her. The words jumbled in her mind as Hunter pushed in closer and dipped his head. His lips scrapped against her ear as he asked again, "Why can't I be your mate, Lily? Am I not good enough for you?"

She turned her head, breathing in his scent. He smelled of the change in the seasons, spring on the verge of summer. Lily lost her goddess-driven mind once more and her tongue darted out to lick his neck. He tasted like home. She felt it in her bones, down in her core, and within her bloodstream. Everything he was and what they could be together filled her mind, and she felt a shift within her.

A spark of something buried deep, a lingering taste of magic.

Hunter groaned and pushed her against the door, and she could feel his hard erection between them. "Little Witch..." he rumbled and trailed a hand up her spine and neck, grasping her hair. He tilted her head slightly, and Lily angled her lips against his.

She opened her mouth, the kiss deep and claiming from the second their lips touched. Her entire body hummed to life. Electricity shot through her, and the sounds of fireworks burst through her mind. Hunter's hands slid down her spine to grasp her bare thighs. He lifted her up and Lily wrapped her legs around his waist. Somewhere in the back of her mind, Lily knew she needed to come up for air. That anyone could walk by right now and catch them mouth fucking each other on the entryway door.

Instead, she wrapped her hands around Hunter's neck, gripping his hair. Her hips moved of their own accord in slow, agonizing circles, rubbing her core against Hunter's straining erection. He matched her pace and the electricity running through her veins cascaded outwards. She felt the shock wave ripple through her every nerve ending, searing her lips. It felt good, too good. Lily broke the kiss first, needing to think through her lust-filled mind. Hunter growled and Lily groaned in response. The growl tugged at some primal instinct deep inside of her, and she wondered if he would growl like that between her legs. Hunter leaned down, nipping along her neck to her collarbone. Her breath hitched and Lily tugged at Hunter's hair.

Lily muttered a curse and yanked harder until Hunter finally looked at her. The intensity of his eyes burned her all the way down to her toes. She was ready to give everything to this Lycan she barely knew, and that thought alone should have scared her. As she searched his eyes, Hunter did the same. She leaned in to kiss him again, to tell him he could chase her under the moon, when a very pointed cough broke into the moment between them.

Chapter Five

Hunter

Hunter couldn't think.

His entire body hummed with static electricity, and his skin felt too tight. The witch in his arms was all soft skin and breathless moans. He could smell her arousal, yet she resisted him, her mind trying to find the logic behind the mate bond fighting to tether them together. Then she licked his neck, and he became unhinged. He kissed her with as much ferocity as he could manage. Claiming her as his mate in the only way she would understand. She just had to trust him.

He heard the fireworks going off outside, signaling that the chase would be starting soon, but he couldn't think about that. All he could concentrate on was his little witch in his arms, with her thick thighs wrapped around his waist. He had her pushed up against the main door, his thick erection grinding against her wet pussy.

She moved her hips in tandem with his, and he had to physically restrain himself from unzipping his pants and plunging his cock inside of her.

Fuck. His little witch, his fate-given mate, already had him wrapped around her delicate fingers. He would follow her like a good fucking wolf to the ends of the world if that was what she wanted. He growled as she broke the kiss, and Hunter started kissing and nipping around her neck. She pulled at his hair, squirming in his grasp. Finally, his little witch yanked hard enough to pull his head up. Their gazes connected, and he fell even harder into the deep chasm of her enchanting eyes. Her gaze seared him down to his bones and into the entire fabric of his being.

And he saw it in her eyes.

His little witch was about to give in. She wanted this just as much as he did. She was going to say yes to him, to this, to their mating bond.

Hunter leaned in for another kiss, just as a very loud and very annoying cough interrupted the moment.

He was going to murder whoever had just interrupted them, very... *very* slowly, with lots and lots of torture. A growl reverberated from his chest, and he bared his teeth before glancing over his shoulder.

His sister coughed into her hand and shrugged. He wanted to wipe that stupid shit-eating grin off her face as Lily squirmed in his grip again. He loosened his hold, allowing her to slide down his body to the floor. "What do you want, Sasha?"

Hunter's sister clapped her hands together and pointed at him and his little witch. "This I like. You two look adorable together. Butttt..."

She trailed off, and Hunter whistled through clenched teeth. "It's about to start, and I need to give the fucking speech, don't I?"

Sasha nodded and glanced over his shoulder expectantly at Lily. Hunter followed her gaze to his panting witch. She gulped, her beautiful rose-pink blush covering her chest and face. Lily shook a curtain of ruby-red hair over her face and mumbled something about needing some air. Her hand clawed at the doorknob, and Hunter rested his hand over hers. He opened the door for her, showing his little witch she wasn't trapped.

Glancing up at him, her hazel eyes darkened as they roamed over his face. She had been so quick to get away from him after their kiss, yet the look in her eyes made it seem like he was rejecting her. He leaned down and rested his forehead against hers. "Get your air, my little witch. But please don't leave. At least not without saying goodbye first."

She blinked quickly and broke contact, taking a wobbling step outside before turning to look back at him. "I... I won't leave," she stammered before shutting the door in his face.

That simple act alone equally ripped out Hunter's heart and made his stomach flutter with happiness. She wasn't going to leave. His little witch was just right outside. She hadn't rejected him, even if she did just shut the door in his face.

Hunter cracked his neck before straightening his tie and shirt. His mate had managed to untuck it with her hold on him. He chuckled, knowing that if their make-out session had lasted even a moment longer, he would have lost control and rutted her right against the door. For some reason, Hunter thought his sexy little witch would like that. "Later," he murmured as he licked his lips, the taste of her sweet lips against his still lingering. He would fuck her good and long against the door later... and probably the stairs, the wall, on top of the table in the dining room after he thoroughly worshiped her voluptuous body with long licks and—

The annoying laughter of his guests pulled him out of his dirty thoughts, and he snapped his eyes up to his still-waiting sister. She was looking at the ceiling, humming lightly and rocking on her heels. "Go watch my mate," he growled and pointed out the door.

Sasha snapped her head down and growled right back, "Is there a *please* attached to that order, Brother?"

Her eyes flashed with fury as she met his gaze; the only other Lycan in this house who had the power to do so. He breathed deeply, but held her gaze. "Please, Sister. I am on the edge right now. You know I mean no disrespect."

The fury slipped from her eyes, and she glanced away, before sighing with much more drama than needed. "Fineeeee, but hurry up. There is a sexy little blonde inside that I have had my eyes on for a bit. I've been slowly working my wiles on her, and I think she will let me chase her instead of the brutish Lycan male she came with."

Hunter barked out a laugh as she stalked past him and dramatically opened the door. She yelled, "Lilyyyyy, wait for meeeeee."

He shook his head before stalking back into the party to deliver a speech and make sure everything was in order for the chase.

Then he would get back to his own personal chase and convince his beautiful mate that this thing between them was very much real and everlasting. And once he did, he was never going to let her go.

Chapter Six

Lily

Lily stared at the slightly pinkish moon in the sky and sighed. She wanted to kick off her shoes, strip naked, and bathe in the gorgeous moonlight to calm her racing mind. She didn't know why, as she had never actually bathed in the moonlight, but she just knew it would calm her down. It was something she always wanted to do but never acted on. Like a lot of things in her life. She always made up some sort of excuse as to why she couldn't. But she knew deep down inside what the real reason was.

She was a fool, a scared fool. In all aspects of her life, even now, her self-proclaimed mate was inside, waiting for her return. And what did she do after almost giving in, after finally stilling her racing mind and seeing that the growing magical bond between them was actually real?

She ran away to sit on an uncomfortable cement step, thinking up lame excuses for why she couldn't be his mate. She didn't even want to think of the remains of magic swirling inside of her from the kiss they shared. Something she had all but given up on ever feeling.

A mate and magic waited for her inside, if only she had the nerve to take the first step. Lily's thoughts skittered back and forth until a feminine bellow echoed out into the night. "Lilyyyyy, wait for meeeeee."

The mad clacking of heels running down the steps interrupted her thoughts as Sasha plopped down next to her with a large grin plastered across her face. Lily shied away, not wanting Hunter's sister to see the doubt clouding her mind. "Did my m..., er, Hunter send you to watch me?"

Lily had almost slipped, calling Hunter her mate. It already felt so natural and good. So why was she fighting so hard against it? Sasha snorted at her almost slip but didn't call her out on it.

"My brother is inside making sure part two of this shindig starts rolling. Speaking of which, are you going to do it?"

Lily blinked. "Do what?"

"The chase and accept my brother as your mate."

Her eyes grew wide at the question, her mind already spitting out reasons why she couldn't, even as her body turned to mush just thinking about it. Sasha held up her hand before Lily was able to speak. "How about this... tell me what you are worried about. Ask *me* all your burning questions and maybe my answers can easy your mind."

Lily felt a bit of weight lift off her chest and nodded. She asked the one question that had been skittering across her mind from the start. "Do I have a choice?"

Sasha's face softened, her grin falling into a slight lip tilt. She reached out to grab Lily's hand. "Of course, you do. You can walk away right now. You don't have to accept the mate bond."

Lily felt the sweet rush of relief pass through her. She had a choice. She could walk away. That was, until she thought about Hunter going out and mating with another woman. Jealousy bloomed throughout her, and she had to push it down.

She needed to get a grip on her emotions. One minute, she wanted to run away and, the next minute, she was more than willing to throw hands at anyone who dared touch her mate.

She closed her eyes and took a deep breath. Fuck, it was getting harder and harder to not think about Hunter being her mate. "What is the mating bond, exactly?" she asked. "Is it just a breeding thing? Or is it something more?"

Sasha laughed. "No, it isn't some sort of breeding thing. The mate bond is something much more; it is the connection to your other half. A ying and yang of sorts. Stars that shine brighter when they are together."

Lily glanced at Sasha out of the corner of her eye as the Lycan female's voice softened and cracked. She was staring up at the stars, eyes glistening before shaking her head and caught Lily looking at her. She saw something flash behind Sasha's eyes, something broken and bruised. Reaching out, she grabbed her hand. "Are you okay?"

Sasha took a deep breath and smiled weakly. It was a stark contrast to the confident woman Lily had experienced earlier. "Don't worry about me. This is about you and my brother. What do you feel deep down inside of you? Focus on that."

Lily gulped and did as Sasha said. She focused on the burning feeling in her heart, the understanding flowing through her veins. She had to trust her intuition, and her intuition was screaming at her that everything would work out better than she could ever dream.

Sasha straightened and stood, her demanding presence back in full force, her metaphorical armor sliding back into place, and Lily focused her gaze back to the Lycan female. "A mate bond doesn't happen to everyone. It's rare enough to be special, but you still need to choose. Because when the mate bond snaps into place, there is no undoing it. Our Alpha, my brother, is a good person. And our pack is a lot more progressive than others. You being a witch doesn't matter to us. Not like that dick face from before. We aren't like that. Even if you weren't my brother's mate, he would have intervened. Honestly, I was about to intervene before my brother all but tackled you."

Tears welled in Lily's eyes at her words. Everything about this was alien and strange, yet... it didn't feel that way. Sasha and Hunter already felt like coming home and sitting down in front of a toasty fire after walking miles through a snowstorm. She couldn't explain the feeling, just that it was right. She took a deep breath and nodded.

Sasha beamed down at her and extended her hand. "Is that a yes, then?"

Fear and doubt still tugged at Lily, trying to cloud the feelings in her heart, but she buried them and reached out. Sasha pulled her into a standing position and waited for Lily to answer her question.

"Yes."

Sasha's grin glinted against the moonlit as she tugged Lily back up the stairs and into the foyer. Yet instead of heading back into the main party room, she tugged her to the left and toward the stairs. "Let's get you into something much more suited to running through the woods."

"Welllllll, it's *technically* more comfortable," Lily muttered while looking this way and that in the long mirror. She was dressed in a ridiculously short, black, silky slip. She could clearly make out her hard nipples through the fabric, and her booty was a hairsbreadth away from being revealed. Sasha was still clambering around in the large closest of the bedroom she had dragged Lily into.

Lily frowned and adjusted the silly rabbit ears still on her head. Sasha had insisted on keeping them on. Something about looking like a tasty little snack...

"Fuck ya," Sasha yelled, and a pair of shoes flew across the room, hitting the floor with a thump. She emerged a second later with a cheeky smile on her face. "Let's go, let's go. Don't wanna be late."

Lily tugged at the slip and sat down on the bed, reaching for the shoes, whilst trying to keep the slip from riding up. Sasha snorted at her struggles before rushing over to help. "Are you sure there isn't anything longer in the closest I could wear?"

Sasha shrugged. "Well, you wouldn't go with my naked idea, so no."

"I'm not prancing around butt ass naked with all these people around. Oh..."

"Oh, what?"

Fear wrapped its way up her spine for a moment. "The other Lycan guy won't be there, do you think?"

Sasha snorted and shook her head. "Hell no. Hunter kicked him out of the house immediately. He is long gone, probably running home to his rich daddy with his tail quiet literally tucked between his legs."

Lily sighed in relief before panic gripped her heart and she lunged across the bed, snatching up her purse and pulling out her cell phone. Her hands shook violently, and Sasha grabbed her hands.

"Lily, what wrong? I can smell your terror suddenly. If you don't want—"

"No... no, it's Silina. She... she... she was waiting at the gates in a car. What if he attacked her because he was angry about..."

Tears hazed her vision and Sasha grabbed the phone from her hands. "Breath, Lily... Breath. We have security cameras pointed out that way. We would have been alerted if anything happened."

Lily gulped as Sasha put her phone back in her hand and scrolled through her contacts until Silina's name came up. She whispered a silent thank you as she pushed the call number.

Silina picked up on the third ring. "You okay, Lily? Need me to pick you up?"

Lily closed her eyes, and sighed heavily. "No, no, I just wanted to make sure you were safe. You aren't still waiting, right? You left?"

"Ya, I went to a coffee shop down the road. But I can be there in five minutes if you need me."

"No need, I'll be here... for a while still."

A long silence greeted Lily, and she pulled the phone away to make sure the call didn't drop. "Silina?"

A rough chuckle finally came over the line. "You are staying past midnight?"

Lily gulped. "Yes."

Silina laughed again. "You dirty little horn dog, I love you. Get some and stay safe. Call me in the morning."

With her parting words, the line went dead, and Lily bit her lip, doubt starting to keep in again. Sasha patted Lily's thigh before hauling her up to standing and grabbing her hand. "Okay, your friend is fine and seems approving of you staying here. So enough muttering and whining. If you keep it up, I'm going to throw you over my shoulder and chase you through those woods myself."

Lily gave Sasha the once-over and almost... *almost* said she would like to see her try. But she really only wanted one person to chase her through the woods, and that was Hunter. She took another deep and stabilizing breath, pushing the keeping doubt away. Lily knew if she didn't go through with this, she would regret it for the rest of her life. She motioned to the door, "Fine, Fine, let's go."

Sasha squealed and clapped her hands before herding Lily out the door and down the stairs.

Chapter Seven

Lily

"Everyone is already outside," Sasha muttered as she kicked off her high heels at the sliding glass door leading to the massive backyard. The woods beckoned silently, pushing up against the well-manicured lawn. A small group of guests stood on the lawn in various states of undress and Lily searched for Hunter among the group. Her heart squeezed, anxiety pooling through her body when she couldn't find him.

"Where is he?" she hissed before realizing Sasha wasn't next to her anymore.

A strong arm encircled her waist from behind, and Lily crashed into a hard chest with a squeak. She grabbed the man's bare forearm and looked up. Hunter's gaze caught hers and his eyes pierced her down to the depths of her soul. Lily whimpered and squeezed her thighs shut, her pussy already going slick from just his penetrating gaze.

Oh, goddess above, she should not have thought of the word penetrate. Her pussy clenched at the thought of something else of his penetrating her.

"Where is who?" he rumbled before dipping his head and nipping at her lips. He squeezed Lily even tighter when she nipped his lips back.

"You," she breathed out before turning in his grasp, burying her hands into his short hair and standing on her tiptoes. His eyes widened slightly at her boldness, then he chuckled.

"Little Witch, I have a feeling you will be forever surprising me."

Lily smiled at his words and kissed him. Hunter tucked her against his body, hand tangling in her hair as he deepened the kiss. Lily wasn't sure how long they stood there, exploring each other's mouths.

Suddenly, Hunter broke the kiss, and Lily gasped as his eyes flashed amber. He sucked in a deep breath and an involuntary shiver ran down Lily's spine as he rumbled. He loosened his hold on her and only then did Lily glance around. They were all alone on the lawn. Her ears picked up the sound of squeals of delight and groans from within the forest. She bit her lip as she watched Hunter begin to shed his clothes. He winked at her. "This is where you run, Little Witch, and I chase you. Unless you want me to fuck you right here on the damn lawn."

Lily froze, thinking it over until she grinned like an idiot. No, she wanted this Lycan, her mate, to chase her.

She took off running, avoiding the sounds coming from the other couples in the woods. She headed away from the sounds, feet pounding hard against the damp forest floor. There were small trails weaving this way and that. Some made by animals and others by people. Lily sprinted down one of the smaller paths before veering to the left. A pull deep in her gut had her weaving between the trees, abandoning the footpath she was on until she spilled out of the trees into a small meadow decorated with a myriad of wildflowers. She paused, breathing harshly, as the moonlight spilled over her. A low growl emanated from the woods, and Lily turned. A wolf prowled toward her, and Lily's heart pounded in her ears.

Moon beams glinted over its silver and white fur as it stalked closer, corralling Lily farther into the small meadow. She really hoped this was Hunter and not some other random wolf. Her breath caught as shimmering fog started at the wolf's feet, slowly swallowing its entire body. Between one breath and the next, Hunter emerged from the shimmering fog, shadows and moonlight playing over his rugged features.

Lily's gut clenched, arousal spreading through her entire body all the way down to her toes. He prowled closer and Lily's chest heaved, nipples already puckering through the thin fabric. She took a step back and stumbled. Lily shut her eyes on instinct, knowing she was about to hit the ground hard. Except the fall never came, as strong arms engulfed her body. She snapped her eyes open to stare into Hunter's glowing orbs. She felt his muscles tense against hers as he slowly lowered both their bodies to the ground. His jaw clenched, nostrils flaring. His movement was stiff as he pushed her stray hairs out of her face and behind Lily's ear. "Do you really want this? Because once we mate, there is no going back. It's for life. I promise it will be a good life, but you still have the choice to walk away."

The words seemed to rip from Hunter's throat, and Lily realized then why he was so tense. He was fighting himself and the bond, still trying to give her a chance to take things at a normal pace. Except Lily had discovered something between walking into the party hours earlier to this moment.

Lightning coursed through her veins, and she knew somehow finding her mate had unlocked her magic, and with it a newfound confidence in herself. She pushed her chest into his, arching her back. Hunter groaned and leaned into her, hands digging into the soft earth next to her hips.

Lily whispered, "I want you. Claim me as your mate."

Hunter's mouth was on hers in an instant, hands at her thighs, pushing the thin fabric farther up and her legs open wider. Lily gasped as calloused fingers glided gently over her throbbing pussy. She was already so wet and ready for him. Lily shifted, trying to get closer to his fingers, desperately wanting them inside of her. She shifted her grip on his shoulders, hands roaming down the muscles over his sides until she got to his erection. He had shed all his clothing to chase her through the woods, and they both groaned as Lily squeezed his thick cock.

"Fuck, Little Witch," Hunter murmured as he broke their kiss, and Lily continued to stroke his shaft. She had to admit it, she really liked it when he called her Little Witch.

"Say it again," she whispered, and rubbed her fingertips over the tip of his cock.

"Fuck, Little Witch, just like that."

She smirked and lifted her fingers to her mouth. They were covered in pre-cum, and she moaned as her tongue darted out to clean them. Hunter growled low and deep, watching her suck on her fingers before lunging forward and pressing her into the dirt. He pushed her hand away and captured her lips with his again. The sound of tearing fabric echoed through the small meadow. Lily shivered as Hunter laid his bare body against hers, fingers twining through hers and shoving her hands overhead. The tip of his cock nudged at her drenched entrance and Lily lifted her hips as Hunter pushed into her.

Lily gasped as Hunter's cock filled her to the brink, burying himself in one long thrust. His grip tightened on her hands as he slowly pulled out and slammed back into her once again. She arched her back, heels digging into the soft ground beneath her as Hunter continued his slow and deep rhythm. Breaking the kiss, she cried out. She was on the edge of an orgasm and her magic flared out around them. The ground crackled with electricity, nipping at her skin. Hunter released her hands to grip the back of her neck and hair. "Little Witch," he murmured against her skin. "Look at me."

She opened her eyes, locking her gaze with his as Hunter moved over her. His skin glowed with the light of the moon, his eyes like living flames. She gripped his shoulders hard as her orgasm started to roll through her. Lily cried out as Hunter continued his thrusts, her pussy pulsating around his cock. He trailed kisses down her neck until he got to her shoulder. She felt him open his mouth, teeth cold against her bare skin before he bit down. When her skin split beneath his bite, instead of pain, all Lily felt was overwhelming pleasure. As she bucked her hips against his, her orgasm crested to new heights. The ground became electrified, static prickling at her skin, and then she felt it. A bond growing tight between her body and his. She could feel it with her magic. A tether linking the two of them together.

Hunter groaned as her pussy continued to milk his cock. He lost his rhythm, and three thrusts later, she felt him coming inside of her. Lily shivered in his arms and wrapped her legs around Hunter's waist as he rested his warm body against hers. All she could hear was the rapid beating of their two hearts, so in sync, they sounded almost one. Hunter licked the bite he had given her before trailing light kisses across her jaw to her lips. Her pussy gave his softening cock one last squeeze before he slipped out of her. She sighed against his soft kisses. "That felt... that was..."

Lily trailed off, unsure of how to explain the feeling of the mate bond between them and how her newly found power felt coursing through her veins. Hunter rumbled against her skin. "Electrifying?"

Scoffing, she felt his lips quirk up in a smile against her skin. He rolled away, taking Lily with him until she rested half over his chest. She snuggled into the crook of his arm and glanced at the dark sky above them. The moon was unwavering in its glow, bathing them in silver moonlight. Lily could finally feel the power and magic flowing out of it, could feel it coursing through her. She lifted her hand, floating it through a moonbeam until Hunter reached up and grasped her fingers. When she glanced back at him with a smile, he trailed kisses over her fingertips. Sighing, she rolled over on top of him, and Hunter chuckled, his cock growing hard between them once more.

Chapter Eight

Hunter

Fuck, his mate was gorgeous.

Hunter grasped her hips as Lily rolled on top of him and placed her hand over his thumping heart. His cock hardened between her warm thighs as she bit her lip and glanced down at him with her beautiful hazel eyes. He could feel the mate bond settling between them and grunted in satisfaction. A sparkle of mischief flowed through the bond, and Hunter smirked as his mate reached up to remove the rabbit ears still somehow gracing her head. She placed them on him and giggled. "Looks like this little witch caught a big, bad rabbit."

A blush formed across his mate's cheekbones, and she shifted slightly across his hard cock. Embarrassment flowed down the bond after her words, and he growled when she went to remove the ears she had put on him.

"Don't you dare touch the bunny ears. They are mine now."

His mate paused, conflicting emotions flowing down their new bond. In the end, it settled into playful suspicion. Lily placed her palms lightly on his chest and wiggled her well-proportioned ass over his hips. Her pussy lips glided over his cock, and Hunter groaned. "Little Witch, my mate, are you trying to tease me?"

Lily bit her lip and shrugged, causing her ruby-red hair to tumble over her shoulder. Hunter felt doubt slowly creep down the bond and he sat up, placing a finger under his mate's chin. She stilled, her beautiful eyes connecting with his. "Do you feel it? The bond between us?"

Lily nodded slightly, and Hunter smiled.

"Now tell me, what do you feel exactly?"

He pushed everything he was feeling down their bond and watched as Lily's eyes widened and her pupils dilated. He felt her pussy dampen against his cock as he pushed his lust for her down the bond. She took a shuddering breath as Hunter dropped his hand to her neck, fingers trailing over the mating bite mark binding them together at the height of their orgasms. His hand trailed lower until he got to her plump breasts. He pinched and rolled her nipples slightly, and she arched into his hand before he dropped it even lower.

Her hips jerked as he skimmed her clit, and her fingernails bit into his shoulders. Lily moaned and rolled her hips against his cock in an intoxicating rhythm. He continued his strokes on her clit as he leaned in to nip at her jaw. His mate angled her face down to capture his lips.

"That's it, Little Witch. Tease me just like that," he murmured against her mouth before deepening the kiss. He could feel her magic surrounding them, building like a wave in the air and nipping at his skin. The forest floor around them radiated with electricity and Hunter broke the kiss quickly as he felt the immense pleasure from his mate flow down the bond. She was about to come, and he wanted to be inside of her. She must have had the same idea as she broke their kiss and pushed his chest, laying him down. He willingly submitted to her, the only person in the world who would ever have that type of power over him.

Hunter moved his hands to her hips, pulling Lily up slightly so his cock could align with her dripping entrance. He eased her down slowly, despite her wanting to slam herself onto him. He grinned as his mate whimpered and begged for more.

"I need all of you," Lily moaned and scraped her fingernails along his chest. Hunter tightened his grip and lifted her up his shaft slightly. A growl worthy of any Lycan spilled out from his mate's throat. "Hunter, please!"

He felt her magic pulse around them, her pussy starting to grip around the tip of his cock, and loosened his hold on her hips. She slid down his shaft easily, her pussy tightening at the very end, and Hunter groaned as

Lily screamed in pleasure. Her pussy milked his cock, shuddering and pulsating as he pulled out and slammed into her again. He wasn't going to last much longer, not with his goddess of a mate riding him through her orgasm. Her magic broke, exploding around them and lighting up the night.

Hunter came with a growl two thrusts later, holding himself deep within his mate. Lily sighed and stretched, holding her arms up toward the moon. Hunter's cock twitched inside of her and, in response, her pussy squeezed around him. As his mate glanced at him, pure bliss painted across her face. Her eyes seemed glazed over and Hunter reached up, placing a hand on her cheek. "So beautiful," he murmured, and his mate giggled.

She turned her head, kissing the palm of his hand before sliding forward to lay on his chest. He wrapped his arms around her, gliding his fingers up and down her spine as she kissed the side of his neck. They lay like that, aimlessly caressing each other, until Hunter's cock went soft and slipped out of her soft pussy. Her breathing had deepened, tranquility flowing down their bond, and Hunter thought her asleep until she murmured almost too low for him to hear.

"So, now what?"

Hunter tightened his hold on her. "What do you mean, Little Witch?"

Lily turned her head and wiggled her body to the side. She stared up at the slowly lightening sky instead of at him and he felt uncertainty twist down their mating bond. She rubbed absentmindedly at the mating mark on her neck. When she didn't say anything, Hunter tucked her in closer to his side. "I'm not going to..." He stopped. "No, let me restart."

She snuggled in closer as Hunter struggled with his words. "Well... I mean, being mated is like... it's like being..."

He glanced over at Lily's big hazel eyes staring at him, waiting patiently, and his mind went blank. "I'll be yours. Happily yours for as long as you will have me."

Lily smiled softly and rested her hand on his chest. "I get that. I was just wondering, like, what now? Do we... date? Instantly move in together. What about your pack? Will they accept me? And what about my powers?"

Her voice took on a higher pitch, panic filtering down their bond, and she sat up, flinging out her hands. "Oh, my Goddess! Look at what I did while we were having sex."

She pointed to the slightly charred earth surrounding them.

Hunter threw his head back in laughter and grabbed Lily to his chest. He couldn't stop laughing as she grumbled against him. "It's not funny. I could have electrocuted you to death."

He hiccupped, wiping at the tears building in his eyes, and managed to suck in a breath. "Lily, baby. Fuck. When I die, I pray it's from having sex with you. Please ride me to the gates of death."

She tried pushing away from him, annoyance running down their bond. She nipped at his neck hard enough to bruise, which only made Hunter start to laugh again. His mate wrestled against him until she started laughing with him. Soon their laughter died off naturally, and Hunter rubbed his mate's back gently. "Little Witch, we can do all those things if you want. We can go as slow as you want."

Lily sat up and scrunched her nose. "Really?"

Hunter sat up with her and tapped his mate's nose gently. "I will take you out on as many dates as you want. I can move in with you or the other way around. I will follow you anywhere you want to go. And my pack *will* love you, so don't you worry about that. And as far as your powers go, I will do everything I can to make sure you can control them. And when you want to go scorched earth again while having sex, or call down the biggest lightning storm anyone has ever seen, you better be riding me through it all."

Lily bit her bottom lip as tears pricked at the corners of her eyes. Warm emotions of love and acceptance rolled down their bond, and Hunter wanted to bask in the feeling. He reached out, cupping her face. "It's you and me forever. You never have to doubt that."

She sniffled before wiping her eyes and reaching out to grab the bunny ears that had fallen off during their last sexcapade. Putting them on her head, she gave him a shy smile. "You promise?"

"Always, my little witch."

His mate shifted, coming to her knees before standing. His hand slipped away from her, and Hunter smirked.

Lily took a small step back and winked at him. "Chase me home, then."

She took off in a run, words barely registering in Hunter's mind, and he leapt to his feet. His shift was seamless, human to wolf in the blink of an eye. His eyes glinted in happiness, the love of his mate radiating down their bond as she turned to see if he was following.

He sprinted after his little witch, through the woods, and back home.

And Hunter knew this would be one chase he would never get enough of.

Chapter Nine

Six Months Later - Lily

Lily peeked inside the small office room and frowned. The light on the desk was barely enough to illuminate her mate and the papers scattered all over the place. She had been looking for him all over the house for the last hour. She should have known he would still be in his office, pouring over the proposal her coven and high priestess were going to present to the council of supernaturals in the next couple of weeks. Her heart almost burst at the seams with happiness as she stared at him.

Hunter. Her mate.

She quickly caught the feeling before it floated down their mate bond. She had been practicing along with her other magic and it seemed to work because Hunter didn't raise his head. Silently padding over the carpet, she came up behind him. He was still staring at the proposal and highlighted a sentence before rubbing his eyes.

"Hey, Little Witch. I know it's late. I hope you didn't stay up..."

He trailed off as Lily let one simple, yet effective feeling roll down their bond.

Lust.

The chair squeaked as Hunter turned around slowly, and his eyes lit up as Lily let the robe she was wearing float to the ground.

"Lily," Hunter growled as she crawled into his lap and grabbed his hands to place on her ass.

He fisted the black and white silk slip she was wearing and pulled her closer. His eyes raked over the thin material covering her breasts all the way up to the bunny ears she had donned just for the occasion.

Leaning in, she kissed him. Her mate opened his mouth instantly and Lily deepened the kiss. She threaded a hand through his hair and gripped the back of his neck with her other. Hunter slid his hands under her ass and lifted, sitting her on the desk in one fluid motion without breaking the kiss. As his hands roamed her body, Lily arched into him as he cupped her breasts. He pinched her nipples through the thin material before one of his hands slid lower. Her legs were already wide, and Hunter growled into her mouth when he discovered nothing between his hand and her pussy.

She broke the kiss and smirked at her mate. Hunter's eyes gleamed, and he licked his lips. "You know I didn't forget; I just got a little sidetracked."

Lily faked a pout. "Oh really? Because here I thought you forgot our six-month anniversary. Thought I had to get creative for you to remember." She pointed to the bunny ears.

A rumble echoed from Hunter's chest as his fingers tickled at her entrance. "I would never forget the date my mate came barreling into my life."

Hunter pulled away, and Lily murmured in protest. Her mate winked at her before falling to his knees and throwing her thighs over his shoulders. She grabbed his hair, tilting his head up, and Hunter gave her a wolfish smirk. "Is my big, bad wolf gonna eat bunny for dinner?"

Hunter grinned and shoved his face between her legs, licking her pussy all the way from top to bottom before circling her clit. Lily moaned, eyes rolling back as her mate continued to lick her core. Her magic started to swell, electricity humming around them. As her mate lavished her pussy with his tongue, Lily relaxed into the feeling, pleasure and magic mixing into one.

Hunter's hands gripped her ass, pulling her closer onto his face, and she groaned. She started to pant, and Hunter growled, the vibrations making Lily arch her back. When he pulled back and nipped at her clit, Lily's grip on his hair tightened as lightning lit up the night sky outside the window. Her orgasm came swiftly, and she cried out, magic whipping the papers off the desk and onto the floor.

The electricity flickered, and Lily fell back, breathless, against the office desk. Hunter gave her pussy one last lick before standing up. He reached up and plucked the ears from her head and, with a smirk, put them on himself. Lily snorted in laughter, which quickly turned into a moan as Hunter hooked one over her legs over his shoulder. The angle lifted her ass off the desk slightly and she held her breath as he unzipped his jeans. His cock nudged at her entrance, and he teased her with his tip. She squirmed against him, needy pants filling the electrically charged air. Her magic nipped at him, and Hunter shivered, his eyes hooding from the feeling.

Lily knew he liked it when she used her magic on him; he had told her as much on their first night together. His cock grew even harder at her entrance when she let her magic flow across his skin again. He slowly pushed into her, and Lily squirmed, wanting him to go faster.

"Always so impatient, my little witch."

Lily moaned and tried to buck her hips against his, but he held her in place. When he started to pull out, Lily nipped at him hard with her magic. He stilled and shivered slightly as her magic rolled over him again, wrapping its way over Hunter's entire body.

She gripped his cock with her pussy, and he growled as she sent a tingling shock wave into his cock. He threw his head back, jaw grinding down, and Lily knew she had won. His control snapped and Hunter slammed his hips forward, burying his cock deeper inside of her. Continuing his onslaught, he drove deeper with every thrust. His moans grew louder, mixing with his wild growls. Soon her magic released with a loud crack and crashed over them at the same time as they orgasmed together. The popping sound of a light bulb breaking caught both their attention and Lily giggled.

Hunter snorted and shook his head before releasing one of his hands from her hip. He pulled open the top drawer of his desk and took out a new lightbulb. His eyes glowed in the dark as he tossed the broken bulb into the trash and spun the new one onto the desk lamp. "Hmmm... I need to work harder next time."

Lily tilted her head in confusion as her mate took a step back and slid out of her.

"I don't understand. Work harder at what?"

Hunter gave her a lust-filled look. "I'm obviously not working hard enough if I'm only replacing one light bulb. Next time, I'm not stopping until every damn bulb in this house burns up."

It took her a moment to catch up, but when she did, a blush instantly covered Lily's entire body. Her mate had a wicked mind. He winked at her, still wearing those damn bunny ears, and she felt a tug down their mate bond. He wanted to chase her, and she was more than happy to oblige.

She took a few swaying steps back, toward the open office door and the still lit hallway. They were all alone in the estate she now called home, and she knew that they could play their games all night long. Hunter followed her with his eyes, allowing Lily a bit of a head start. She made it to the door before he took his first step forward, and she picked up her pace, taking off down the hallway in a mad dash. She made it all the way to the stairs before strong arms encircled her waist and pulled her into her mate's hard chest. She giggled like a fool as he nipped at her earlobe. She felt him place the bunny ears back on her head, and he whispered, "Tag. Your it, Little Witch."

The weight of his arm around her waist disappeared as Hunter vaulted over the top of the stairs and landed in the entryway of their home. He glanced up at Lily's shocked face and laughed. She gaped at him before growling softly, "You best run, Wolfie, because this rabbit is coming for you."

Lily rushed down the stairs after her mate and followed his laughter through the estate and out to the backyard. She took a deep breath, twirling around in circles, trying to find him. The trees rustled in the suddenly silent night, and she held her breath, reaching down their mate bond. She felt laughter, love, and happiness flowing through it, but couldn't quite pinpoint where her mate was.

He was playing with her, and she smirked.

Fine.

If her wolf wanted to play, she could play too.

She reached deep inside of herself to stir up her newfound magic, and pushed the power down their bond. Normally they had to be touching for her to zap him, but she discovered about a month ago that was no longer the case. She felt surprised on the other end and zapped him lightly again.

Lily snorted when Hunter appeared suddenly from the tree line, leveling a lust-filled stare her way. She zapped him down the bond again and his eyes lit up with carnal fire. He started stalking his way toward her, and Lily met him halfway. His arms encircled her waist, and he was inside of her before they hit the ground. Lily groaned out in pleasure as he bit down over their mating mark on her neck. He slammed his cock over and over inside of her as she kept flowing her power down the bond. Hunter groaned and pulled out of her, only to turn her around. Slapping her ass slightly, he aligned his cock up to her soaked pussy again. "Fuck, Lily. I need to get deeper inside of you," he rumbled, before driving into her with one thrust.

The new angle did exactly that and her eyes rolled back in her head as he started to grind against her slowly, reaching new depths inside her aching pussy. She throbbed around him, coming fast and hard as he reached around to pinch her clit. At the peak of her orgasm, Hunter bit down once more over their mating mark on her neck and Lily's power exploded.

Two thrusts later, Hunter's cock pulsated inside of her, and he collapsed on top of her. She loved how his weight bore down over her like a warm blanket on a cold winter's eve, and she sighed in bliss. He licked at the shell of her ear before reaching a hand around to her chin and tilted her head to the side. She blinked away the fog in her pleasure-hazed mind and stared at the now dark house.

He chuckled and licked the shell of her ear again. Realization had her chuckling along with him. Her mate had fucked her so hard that she blew the entire power out throughout the house. "Maybe I worked a little too hard," he whispered, and Lily frowned.

"Why do you say that?"

"Can you hear it?" he whispered, and Lily strained her ears.

The sounds of dogs howling finally reached her ears, along with the faint sound of car alarms going off. Her eyes widened as she reached out with a spark of power, searching for any electricity in the near vicinity. Her eyes widened when she couldn't feel anything.

She had taken out the electricity within a five-mile radius. Lily started to laugh, and Hunter joined her. They lay there, laughing in each other's arms under the bright moonlight of the night and counted the stars until they slowly winked out of existence and the darkness faded into dawn.

"I love you, my little witch," Hunter whispered and pulled her closer as the sky began to lighten.

Lily snuggled closer in his embrace and gave him a soft kiss. "I love you too, my sexy mate."

The End

Want More?

Are you interested in more of the Wicked Fate, Lusty Mates series ?
What if I told you Carnal Moon is part of a series releasing this year, and the next novella is already up for pre order !
Wild Moon: Releasing February 2024 – Preorder Now
Enchanted Moon: Releasing April 2024 – Preorder Now
Arctic Moon – Releasing June 2024
Feral Moon – Releasing August 2024
Scarlet Moon – Releasing September 2024

Also By Astrid Vail

Wicked Fate, Lusty Mates
Enter a new world of desire with a coven of misfit witches and the steamy discovery of their lycanthrope mates in this brand new series.

Carnal Moon: A Steamy M/F Paranormal Erotic Romance

Wild Moon: A Smoldering M/F Paranormal Erotic Romance

Enchanted Moon: A Second Chance M/F Paranormal Erotic Romance

Arctic Moon – Coming Soon

Feral Moon – Coming Soon

Scarlet Moon – Coming Soon

Holidays After Dark
Winter's Eve: A M/F Fantasy Holiday Short Story

Valentine's Arrow: A M/F Paranormal Holiday Short Story
Fireworks in the Bayou: A M/F Paranormal Holiday Short Story

Courting Sin
Courting Sin : A M/F Devilish Short Story Part One for newsletter subscribers only
Craving Sin: A M/F Devilish Short Story Part Two for newsletter subscribers only

About Astrid Vail

Wild Romance, Epic Adventure – Multi Genre Romance Author
Storyteller at Heart
Born in the backwoods of California, Astrid Vail was raised upon fairytales and fantasy worlds.
With a love of everything otherworldly, Astrid decided to put pen to paper and pull the exotic creatures dancing in her head out into the light of day.
She has been writing professionally since 2022 and has no intention of slowing down anytime soon.
Signup to her newsletter at www.astridvail.com for a free book or two, cover reveals, and all things related to extra spicy book news.

Made in United States
Orlando, FL
25 November 2024